Marian Richardson

The Talk of the Household

Poems

Marian Richardson

The Talk of the Household
Poems

ISBN/EAN: 9783337397760

Printed in Europe, USA, Canada, Australia, Japan

Cover: Foto ©Andreas Hilbeck / pixelio.de

More available books at **www.hansebooks.com**

The Talk of the Household:

POEMS.

BY

MARIAN RICHARDSON.

LONDON:

S. STRAKER & SONS, 26, LEADENHALL STREET.

1865.

DEDICATION.

—

TO WHOM SHALL THIS SMALL TRIBUTE DEDICATED BE?
  So MANY LOVES WITHIN MY HEART HOLD SWAY:
FIRST THOU, MY OTHER SELF, WHOSE STRONG TRUE HEART
  HAS BEEN MY PILOT OVER ALL THE WAY;
THEN YE, DEAR HONORED GUIDES OF EARLY YEARS—
  FATHER AND MOTHER—THRO' WHOSE LOVE WERE SHED
THE SEEDS WHICH SPRINGING INTO LIGHT HAVE STREWN
  THESE LOWLY BLOSSOMS O'ER THE PATH I TREAD;
AND YE, MY CHILDREN, WHO IN AFTER YEARS
  MAY DEARLY PRIZE THESE RECORDS OF OUR DAY
WHEN THEY HAVE SUNK TO SILENCE IN THE PAST,
  AND SHE WHO WROTE THEM MAY HAVE PASSED AWAY.

Lancaster House,
  Peckham Rye.
    July, 1865.

INDEX.

Heroes.

THE World is proud to trace their names
    Upon her ſtoried page,
They are the ſtars whoſe glowing light
    Illumine every age.
Bright from the buried paſt their deeds
    In undimmed luſtre ſhine,
And ſhining on, ſhall ſtill endure,
    Remembered thro' all Time.

Who are they? Lo! a ſolemn crowd
    Comes to the mental gaze
Of Mighty Ones; from Time's young years,
    E'en to theſe later days:

HEROES.

Some who have ftrode with conquering feet
  Through a deep crimfon flood,
And worn at laft a Victor's crown
  Bought with the price of blood.

Some who have given Youth's fair hopes,
  And Manhood's golden prime,
And all life's lateft years to win
  Some treafures for their time.
And fome who fearlefs dared to raife
  Truth's ftandard proud and high
In thofe dark times, when Truth confeffed
  But led them forth to die.

Thefe on the mountain's gilded creft—
  But, lo! the vales below
Bear imprefs of heroic feet
  The World may never know.
For many hidden lives of Toil,
  Obfcure, unfung, unknown,
Shine radiant in the narrow fphere,
  Content, they call their own.

Some who have learned in darkeſt hours
　　To work, and wait for day
With patient hope—tho' clouds and ſtorms
　　Hung over all the way;
Some who have reckoned Duty done
　　An all-ſufficient price—
Some who have triumphed over Self,
　　Nor called it ſacrifice.

For needs it not a hero's heart
　　To chain Ambitions down
To the flow wheels of dull routine,
　　And patiently work on?
To ſee Youth's glittering rainbow dreams
　　Fade ſilently away,
And yet be thankful for the gifts
　　Still ſtrewn upon the way.

To bear through weary days and nights,
　　A boſom's load of grief,
To cruſh the ſorrow down, and find
　　In *Work* its beſt relief;

And even spare a tender hand
    To clear the thorny way,
For bleeding feet, and breaking hearts
    Of wanderers gone astray.

So—tho' to Fame's bright muster-roll
    We lift a reverent eye,
And hope to catch some golden gleams
    To light our footsteps by ;
Yet humbler lives perchance fulfil
    The same divine behest,
And he a *Hero too may be*
    Who nobly does his best.

Common Things.

———

FULL oft the Poet's ſtar-tuned harp
    To noble themes has ſwept the ſtrings,
But mine ſhall take a lowlier ſtrain,
    And ſing the worth of Common Things.

Yes; common things: the daily round
    Of Life's ſmall duties nobly done,
May ſhed more brightneſs o'er the path
    Than ever Poet harped or ſung.

Ye who muſt toil, ſtay not to grieve
    That Labour is your daily lot,
But know your toil-ſtained hands may hold
    Gifts that the rich man knoweth not.

For common toil, well done, may bring
    Reſt ſweeter than might elſe be known;
And ſorrow loſes half its ſting
    When men muſt work the heart-throbs down.

Though far beyond our reach may rife
    Summits we may not hope to gain;
The common path is bright with flowers,
    And Beauty fmiles upon the plain.

For lo! ten thoufand glorious things
    To hearts that feel, and eyes that fee,
Are woven in that wondrous web—
    A Human Life's grand myftery.

For us the funlit morning hours,
    The gold fhed o'er the death of day,
The hufh of eve, the filent night,
    The placid moonlight's filver ray.

And radiant ftars, whofe holy eyes,
    Like angel-watchers of the night,
Look down alike on hut and hall,
    And fhed their calm and peaceful light.

And nearer yet, the lowlieft life
    Some dear heart-treafures may enfold
Tho' common things; Hearth, Home, and Love
    More precious are than gems or gold.

If not for all, for moſt there beams
    The brightneſs of ſome baby-face ;
For moſt there waits ſome kindly ſmiles,
    Some loving words, ſome fond embrace.

We will be thankful then for all,
    And ſeize the bleſſings each day brings,
For ſure life's happineſs diſtils
    Its ſweeteſt drops from Common Things.

Woman's Duties.—Woman's Mission.

———

WOMAN! thou needeſt no glory-wreaths
 To glitter o'er thy name;
'Tis not for thee to hurry on
 In mad purſuit of Fame;
For lo! thou haſt a nobler ſphere
 In that bright ſpot called Home,
Where thou may'ſt reign, and hold ſupreme
 A Queendom all thine own.

What need Ambition be to thee,
 Whoſe taſks, not light or few,
Embrace ambitions high enough
 For thee to battle through;
Not trifling things are Faith and Love
 And ſelf-denying zeal,
And Woman's pride of loſing ſelf
 In other's woe or weal

And not ignoble is thy lot;
　Even in the daily round
Of petty cares and common things
　Some glory may be found.
For duties met and well-fulfilled,
　Bring to a loving heart
A sweeter sense of happiness
　Than aught else can impart.

'Tis thine to cheer the weary one
　When Heart and Hope cast down,
He turns his fainting heart away
　From Life's unpitying frown.
And should the stronger spirit fail
　Of its best inward light,
Thy quick perception, all in love,
　Should gently point The Right.

A thousand-stringèd harp is thine
　To wake the first sweet chords,
When childhood smiles upon thy life,
　And lisps its simple words;

'Tis thine to catch the firſt lit ſmile,
  To mark each baby-grace,
And gently lead the tottering ſteps
  Life's after-path to trace.

No lot ſo lonely, but thou may'ſt
  An influence impart;
The pulſe of Man's more ſtirring life
  If not the Head—the Heart;
In deeds of kindneſs, works of good,
  A helper firm to ſtand;
For Life's ſweet charities to ſtretch
  A ready, willing hand.

This much, and more, is thine; ſo let
  The outſide world in vain
Allure thee from thy ſheltered path
  With Pleaſure, or with Fame.
Hold faſt thy ſilken reins aright,
  Thy quiet life ſhall be
A ſource of bleſſing widely ſpread,
  A crown of light for thee.

Charing Cross.

———

TRUTH ; ours are bufy ftirring times—
 A ftirring, working age—
Scant room there'll be for Soft Romance
 Upon our Hiftory's page.
So mufed I, as with lightning fpeed
 I on my way was borne,
And through the City's mighty midft
 With multitudes fwept on.

On, paft a world of wondrous things
 My curious, gazing eye
Looked on with wonder, almoft awe,
 The fcenes that paffed me by.
Not glories of a bygone age,
 But piles of princely grace,
Where mighty Commerce fits enthroned
 Grand monarch of the place.

The miles of ſtreets, all canopied
    With interlacing wire,
Where the trained lightning waits to work
    At mortal man's deſire;
And the broad river, bridged, and ſpanned,
    Begirt, and overhung,
With wondrous works of ſtrength and ſkill
    Acroſs its pathway flung.

An iron age—all work and noise.
    Yet does my heart not own,
Some glory in theſe ſame great works
    Which crowd our buſy Town?
And feel a throb of grateful pride
    For all the patient toil
Of head, and hand, which thus has reared
    Such trophies on our ſoil.

But 'midſt the wonders—what is this?
    The gazing eye may trace
A ſtructure not ordained for use—
    This croſs of antique grace.

Antique, yet fresh and fair it stands.
    In the bright sunset glow,
To tell the passing crowd a tale
    Of many a year ago.

Of how in ages rough and rude
    True love so bright could shine,
That its warm glow has even reached
    Unto this later time.
And lo! the busy world has paused
    Upon its stern career,
To mark where wept the Soldier King
    Beside the "dear Queen's" bier.

O let the sweet tradition still
    Its pleasant fragrance fling,
And let us feel that faithful love
    Is still a cherished thing;
Not only for the past held dear,
    Is this memorial stone,
Our thoughts fly to our own dear Queen
    Who sits in grief alone.

And as its filent fhadow falls
    Acrofs the crowded way,
The ancient ftory comes again
    Lit by a brighter ray ;
For fhrined in *our* heart of hearts
    Is Albert's memory ;
And *now*, as then, we foftened feel
    True love can never die.

Dead Flowers on a Grave.

AH! ye were bright, when loving hands
   Beftowed ye on the tomb,
Frefh from the garden's ftarry hoft,
   With fummer on your bloom ;
And mourning hearts and weeping eyes
   With fond and gentle care,
Laid the laft offering of their love
   To fade, and perifh there.

They came with memories of a form,
   A loved and cherifhed one ;
A funny fmile for ever pafled,
   A voice of mufic gone.
Methinks I fee their wiftful gaze
   Bent o'er the hallowed fpot,
And catch the broken whifpered words—
   " She ne'er fhall be forgot."

But now, fair flowers, in your dead bloom
   I read a filent tale,
How dearelt memories mult fade,
   And deepelt love mult fail;
A bitter thought might whifper now,
   It is the common lot
To live, to love, and then to die,
   And be at lalt—forgot.

But no! tho' on the crelted waves
   Of forrow fome are borne,
A voice Divine hath fpoken it,
   " Man fhall not always mourn;"
Hands mult not ever folded be
   In mute and paffive woe;
The funfhine cometh after rain,
   And God hath willed it fo.

Still mult Life's common road be trod
   Tho' fairelt things have fled,
And we mult live, and care for ftill
   The Living, not the Dead.

Well that 'tis fo; for One who lulled
 The fleepers to their reſt,
Has loved them more than we can love,
 Therefore, it muſt be beſt.
And lo! for us a filver ſtar
 Pierces the midnight gloom ;
E'en Immortality which fhines
 Triumphant o'er the tomb.

Cobden's Return.

(After the Ratification of the French Treaty.)

———

Rise, Men of Britain—ye who boaſt
    Your Country fair and free,—
The land that reigns in regal pride,
    Crowned Empreſs of the Sea!
Firſt among nations in her power,
    Her liberty, her lore,—
Shout welcome as her Patriot Son
    Regains his native ſhore.
Ye proudly count the noble names
    Of England's Hero-Sons,
Placed high upon the muſter-roll
    Of Earth's exalted ones.
Full oft your thouſand ſpires have pealed
    A Nation's glad acclaim
To thoſe, who, on the field of blood
    Have earned a victor's name:

We honour, too, the true and brave,
    Who, foremoſt in the ſtrife,
For Hearth, and Home, and Liberty,
    Have freely ventured life ;
But o'er their glory comes a cloud,
    Their laurels,—bathed in blood,—
Shine dimly, gliſtening through the tears
    Of ſtricken Orphan-hood.
But now no plumèd Warrior comes,
    No laurels crown the brow
Of *Him*—before whoſe ſense of right
    Have Empires deigned to bow.
A man of peace, yet one who dared
    To hurl his gauntlet down,
And ſtand the "CHAMPION OF FREE TRADE,"
    Fearleſs of ſcorn or frown !
Then welcome him, this earneſt man,
    Whoſe powers of heart and brain,
Whoſe life-long hope has been to this
    Great triumph, to attain—
This "Victor" of a bloodieſs ſtrife
    Who aſks no nobler gain
Than that his " Brother Men" ſhould say,
    " He has not toiled in vain."

His deeds let "Trade and Commerce" tell,
   Whofe flood-gates, opened wide,
For future years rich fpoils fhall bear
   Upon their mighty tide.
His deeds, the League of years gone by,
   Our cheapened daily food;—
Ah! men unborn fhall truly say
   " He worked his country's good."

The Sons of Toil.

—— ——

YE working men, I hold your name
    A title proud to bear,
As his who claims to be the Lord
    Of acres broad and fair.
Your place may be in Life's dim ways,
    Your work obfcure, unknown,
While often clouded o'er with care
    The toiling years pafs on.
What matter tho' the world of wealth
    May never hear your name,
Each working man may hold a place
    The rich can never claim.
Monarchs of toil, whofe ftrength of arm
    And wondrous fkill of hand,
Have crowned with mighty monuments
    Your own beloved land.

Your hearts may glow with honeſt pride,
   To feel that Britiſh ſoil
Owes all its glory and its wealth
   To Britiſh Sons of Toil.
Hard work, hard fare, may be your lot;
   But patience to endure
And courage in the hour of pain
   Are learned through being poor.
The hard-earned cruſt, the lowly roof,
   Great bleſſings though they be,
Are not enough for all your need,
   Nor all that you shall see:
As ye have ſkilful hands to work,
   So ye have hearts to feel,
And heads to think what moſt will make
   Your future woe or weal.
Only to Him who gave you these,
   And to yourſelves be true,
And ye ſhall find what mighty things
   United ſtrength can do.
United ſtriving to ſeek out,
   For all that's pure and good,
Helping each other on the way
   In loving brotherhood.

Rifing above life's meaner things
   To feck a higher goal,
Since ye have learned the deepeft grave
   Can not entomb the foul.
Only have faith—faith in your God,
   And faith in fellow-man,
Faith in your own ftrong earneft will
   To do the beft you can.

Lancashire.

Thou haſt thy rivers broad and bright
   Thy rugged, gorſe-clad fells;
Thy ſhady nooks, thy murmuring ſtreams,
   Thy ſun-lit flowery dells.
And round thee ſtand, like ſentinels,
   Thy mountains grand and hoar;
While ocean's billows foam, and break
   Upon thy pebbly ſhore.

And in thy midſt, like Ethiop-Queens,
   Are cities, ſwarth and grand;
Whoſe work achieves, whoſe wealth upholds,
   The glory of the land.
"Time-honoured Lancaſter," too, holds
   Her "Gaunt's embattled pile,"
Which, grey and grand, ſtill rears its creſt,
   In ancient kingly ſtyle.

But thou haſt more, O Lancaſhire!
   A tale can now be told,
Of greater glory than belongs
   To memories of old.
The times of knightly chivalry
   Have ages paſſed away,
But thou of nobler courage tell'ſt
   In this our modern day:

A tale of brave men nerved to bear
   The bittereſt weight of woe,
With hearts as patient to endure,
   As mortal man may know.
God grant the clouds are paſſing now,
   Which wrapt thee in their gloom;
That never more ſtrong men may ſtarve
   Beſide the ſilent loom.

Thine was the pain, O Lancaſhire!
   Thy country's was the pride!
That Faith and Hope were not o'erwhelmed
   In ſuch a fearful tide.

The nation laid her offering down,
  As friend beſtows on friend ;
The nation thanks the patient hearts
  Which ſuffered to the end.

If haply, never more for us
  The ſnow-white crops ſhall wave;
If peaceful fields and happy homes,
  Become one mighty grave ;
Still o'er the ſea from other lands,
  We hope the welcome ſtore,
And trust that *thou*, brave Lancaſhire,
  Shall pine in want no more.

Earlswood.

———

Not loſt! tho' forth from thoſe dull eye
   No ſoul may ſeem to ſhine,
And though a dark myſterious veil
   Obſcures the light divine;
We must not queſtion Him who made
   His creatures ſo forlorn,
But only uſe love's power to prove
   Not loſt the Idiot-born.

Not loſt! but won to life and hope,
   By patient, gentle care,
Although it be but *one* fair flower
   The poor blank life may bear.
One thought, that God is great and good,
   One hope to gild its way,—
Though but a ſingle ſpark gleams forth,
   'Twill that kind care repay.

So thought a noble toiling man,
   Whofe chofen pathway led
'Midft thofe dark ways where deepeft want
   And darkeft woe are fpread.
He thought, and lo! the princely front
   Of Earlfwood towered to heaven,
Home of as regal charity
   As e'er to woe was given.

He watched it while his life's laft fands
   Were paffing one by one,
Then gently laid him down to die
   Ere yet the tafk was done;
A monument moft coveted,
   A good man's legacy,
Left for his country to maintain,
   And, reader, left to thee.

Man! ftanding proud in giant ftrength
   Of intellect and brain,
O pafs not thefe poor idiots by,
   In all their helplefs pain,

Without a thought, a paufe, a prayer,
   On humble bended knees,
That, but for God's great gift to thee,
   Thou might be fuch as thefe.

Mother! who know'st the heart's deep thrill
   Of grateful, warm delight,
When little eyes beam on thine own,
   Intelligent and bright;
O feel for thefe poor human waifs,
   Caft on life's ftormy tide,
And help the hands which thus have fought
   This fhelter to provide.

This home for which, in earneft voice,
   'Tis charity that pleads,
Sons! Daughters! from your happier fpheres,
   Come, help us in our needs;
That Heaven will fend you recompenfe,
   From whence nor flight nor fcorn,
Nor aught but gentleft pitying love,
   Beholds the Idiot-born.

Kind Words.

—

O THEY are gifts of little coſt,
   But yet of pricelefs worth!
Kind words—I count their tones among
   The precious things of Earth.
Theirs is the Muſic of the Hearth;
   Muſic, whoſe gentle tone
Hath mighty power to make the charm
   Of happineſs at home.

Kind, gentle words! Who hath not felt
   What balm of healing power
Diſtils from their foft influence,
   In Sorrow's darkened hour?
Low whiſpering to the poor, cruſhed heart,
   Hope's precious angel-ſtrain,
That through its tears it may look up
   To Joy, and Peace, again.

Kind Words! Oh ufe them! Thou shalt find
   Them weapons, strong and true,
For work, which Force, and angry threats,
   Perchance, have failed to do.
For they have melted ftubborn hearts;
   And many a wandering one
Has turned upon the downward path,
   By power of kindnefs won.

Great gifts are those of wealth and power;
   But cold and drear 'twould be,
Were they our only drifting fpars
   Upon Life's troubled fea;
For fhining gold doth often fail
   True comfort to impart;
And burning eloquence doth fall
   Coldly upon the heart.

Poor human nature ever craves
   Its meed of human love;
" Love one another," fpake the lips
   Of Him who dwells above.

So let that teaching be our guide :
And when all elfe doth fail
In woe, or sicknefs—we shall find
The power of Love prevail !

After the Pestilence, 1849.

THE shade has fallen on many a hearth,
  And dimm'd the sunlight there;
And hearts which once with joy were full,
  Are breaking in despair.
Voices are hush'd which late had borne
  Life's music on their tone;
And darling ones have pass'd away
  For ever from their home.

Ye, on whose hearts no fick'ning pang
  Has come from Death's swift hands;
Around whose hearth no vacant place
  In desolation stands;
No music hushed, no glad smile pass'd,
  No love and beauty gone—
No tomb sprung up amid your joys
  For you to weep upon.

D

O from the homes fo richly bleſſed
    Let ſongs of praiſe riſe up
In gratitude to Him who ſpares
    The bitter from the cup ;
And 'midſt your yet unwither'd joys,
    Look round on thoſe leſs bleſt ;
And learn, oh, deeply learn to feel
    Pity for thoſe diſtreſs'd.

Ye may not fill the aching void
    Of ſorrow in the heart ;
But gentle words of ſympathy
    At leaſt ſome joys impart.
Tho' myriad gifts are o'er ye flung,
    The beſt that Heaven beſtows
Is that bleſs'd power of ſympathy
    For other's joys or woes.

Look on the Sunny Side.

— —

STAY ; ye who tread Life's chequered path
    With murmuring on the lip,
Who grasp the thorns of every flower,
    Nor stop the sweets to sip,
Grieve not o'er trifles ; this world holds
    Enough of grief beside,
And ye are blest compared to some—
    Look on the Sunny Side.

Stay ; ye so ready to believe
    Ill of your fellow men ;
Are ye then faultless, that ye sit
    In judgment over them ?
None in perfection walk the Earth,
    And faults oft virtues hide ;
Then judge them lightly, if at all,
    And choose the Sunny Side.

The Sunny Side; ah me! to fome
　　Poor forrow-ftricken ones
The words feem fhadows of a time
　　Whofe brightnefs never comes;
Or memories of years gone by,
　　A glad and blithefome ftrain
Of mufic which has blefs'd them once,
　　But ne'er may wake again.

But, though 'tis fo—though o'er your path
　　Sorrows fall thick and faft—
Though love has chilled, and many joys
　　Are buried in your paft—
Though fad, and lone, and defolate,
　　You think e'en Hope denied;
Look up for help, for every life
　　Muft have a Sunny Side!

The Voice of the Fallen.

———

OUR SISTERS! even ye who fweep
   In lofty virtue by,
The curl of fcorn upon your lip,
   And cold, averted eye;
And Brothers, too! whofe mocking jeft
   Is all we dare to claim,
Tho' from your midft *one firft* laid out
   Our wretched path of fhame.

Oh paufe, and pity; woe is ours!
   Woe, dark, abiding, deep,
Though ours are hearts that may not break,
   And eyes which may not weep;
Think not that all our hiftory
   Lies in the practifed wile,
The tinfel garb, the painted cheek,
   The heartlefs, hollow fmile!

Ah no! for *even us* there comes
    Dark flooding o'er the foul,
A tide of mortal agonies,
    Refistlefs, paft control,
Upon whofe waves no glancing light
    Of hope may kindled be,
Nought but the blacknefs of defpair
    And untold mifery.

Yet 'twas not ever thus! far back
    The buried Paft could fhow
Fair budding hopes, too bright, too pure
    To linger with us now;
When joy and innocence, and love,
    And Home's bleft houfehold fhrine,
Bedeck'd with faireft bloffomings,
    Were ours, as well as thine.

But now, our eyes may never meet
    Affection's anfwering gaze—
No hallowed love may crown our life
    Or weep upon our graves—

No hope, no light for such as we
   Sin-stained and sorrow-crushed——
The hard world's unforgiving scorn
   Will keep us in the dust.

Is there no kindly voice to plead
   In Charity's blest name,
No hand stretched forth in such a cause
   To save, to win, reclaim?
No tongue to tell that sin like this
   May hope to be forgiven,
And whisper, " E'en for such as these
   There may be Peace and Heaven?"

For, with some far-off memories
   Of stainless, happy years,
There comes a story lingering still
   E'en in our deafened ears,
Of One who raised a Magdalene,
   Nor spurned her from His door,
But in His holy Temple said—
   " Go forth! and sin no more."

O point the path! fome hearts might turn
    To feek the better way,
And live to blefs the hand which ftrove
    To turn their night to day.
Faint not, tho' hopelefs feem the tafk ;
    Thrice bleft fhall be that hand,
Whofe ftrength was given to wipe away
    A foul ftain from the land.

A Temperance Song.

———

SHOUT, Britain's fons, your Britifh fong,
 Ring forth the noble ftaves,
And found the joyful promife forth,
 Ye never will be flaves.
For though ye fear no foreign foe,
 And own no defpot's thrall,
Ye have a tyrant in your midft
 More cruel than them all.

'Tis Drink, that fierce relentlefs foe,
 Who, in his greed of gain,
Takes youth, and hope, and happinefs,
 And ftrength of arm and brain.
He robs your manhood of its pride;
 Your childhood of it's grace;
And womanhood at his command
 Forgets all pleafant trace.

All gentle love, all tender care,
   All peace of hearth and home,
Are trampled out, defied, forgot,
   Where this fell-fiend has come,
The lives which elfe had fhone fo fair,
   Are withered by his breath,
And know no other end than thefe :
   Madnefs, defpair, and death.

O, fee the ruin of his fway !
   See all the woe, and pain,
In places which were happy homes,
   Till Drink, the tyrant, came,
And ftripped the hearth, once bright and warm,
   The board with plenty fpread,
And clutched with cruel grafping hands,
   The ftarving children's bread.

This is the defpot, brother men,
   O fpurn his cruel chain,
Sure honeft brows will fcorn to bear,
   His burning brand of fhame.

Your fkill of hand, your ftrength of arm,
  Your need of honeft toil,
God gives you for a noble ufe,
  Not for this demon's fpoil.

Then by all happy memories,
  All hopes of joys to come,
Pledge honeft vows that ne'er again,
  His brutifh fway you'll own.
And fing again your noble fong,
  In glad and joyful ftaves,
Happy, and Free ; God helping us,
  " We never will be Slaves !"

The City Missionary.

—

To some t'is given to tread the path,
　Of Glory, and of Fame,
To die ere yet the victor's wreath,
　May bloſſom o'er their name.

And when t'is gained, alas! the meed
　Of long, and toiling years
So longed for, and ſo hardly won,
　Is ſtained with blood, and tears.

A different ſtruggle thine; the fight,
　'Gainſt ignorance, and ſin,
In life's dark ways, unſung, unknown,
　Is yet as hard to win.

The weary days, and anxious nights,
　The efforts oft in vain,
When drear, and hopeleſs ſeems the taſk,
　The loſt ones to reclaim,

Are nobler conqueſt; and a Crown,
 Whoſe glory ſhall not die,
Thou, Soldier of the Crofs may'ſt win,
 For all Eternity.

The Exile's Grave.

'TIS paſt, thy time of ſtrife and pain,
  Thy life's long agony,
And thou art gone where ſtrife ſhall ceaſe,
  And tears be wiped away.
At Reſt—in peace—we leave thee here
  Beneath our Engliſh ſkies,
No longer Exile, in that Heaven,
  Where thy brave ſoul ſhall riſe:
Son of that noble Land, for whom
  Thou would'ſt have died to ſave,
Her tyrants cannot reach thee here,
  Within thy quiet grave.
Our tears avail thee nothing now,
  This ſhall thy requiem be—
The Patriots' ſpirit cannot die,
  And "Poland ſhall be *Free*."

Stanzas.

ART thou ever the fame, with the jeft on thy lip,
   And the light laughter flung on thy mirth-loving
      brow?
Are thy joys, and thy forrows all thofe of the furface,
   Art thou ever as carelefs, as mirthful as now?

I would not thou wert like the Summer-winged rover,
   That lightly from bloffom to bloffom e'er flies;
Tho' its track be the Sunbeam, its flight ever glowing,
   There's no one to weep when the butterfly dies.

Is the light laugh of pleafure enough to entrance thee?
   Does Life yield thee no deeper bleffings than mirth?
Haft thou never yet lived thro' thofe thought-hallowed
     moments,
   Which will raife thee far higher than vifions of Earth.

Pafs on in thy path; may it ever be fhining,
   For fmiles are the Heaven-fent charters of youth;
But Oh! may'ft thou *too* learn to feel, the deep gladnefs
   That wells pure and fweet from the fountain of Truth.

In Memory of the Late S. Gregson, Esq., M.P. for Lancaster.

TOLL deep, toll flow, ye folemn bells!
 Grief's faddeft mufic learn,
For one has journeyed from your midft,
 To never more return.

Full oft and loud ye've welcomed him
 In peals of glad acclaim,
But now ftrike low, and foft, and fad,
 He will not come again.

What tho' he bore the honoured weight
 Of man's allotted years,
His vacant place muft *here* be marked
 With forrow and with tears.

Miffed in yon bufy world where late
 With his compeers he ftood,
Spoke his laft words, ufed his laft powers,
 To labour on for good.

Miſſed there : but thou, oh Lancaſter!
Tenfold the miſs will prove,
For, tho' afar, he may have ſhone
Thou had'ſt his heart of love.

And moſt to thee was that kind voice,
That pleaſant, kindling eye ;
That "good, grey head," which never paſſed
Unmarked, unhonoured, by.

How oft, when wearied with the ſtrife,
He came for peace and reſt,
And found them in the quiet ſcenes
He ever loved the beſt—

Thy moor, thy river, and thy hills,
Thy crag-encircled ſea,
And far beyond, thy ſilent peaks
Riſing in majeſty.

Theſe loved he—but not only theſe,
His kind and generous heart
Turned to the people of the place,
And filled a brother's part.

E

No grander monument can be
    Than that raifed by his hands,
The fane which on yon moorland-fide,
    In facred beauty ftands.

And many another work of love
    Will long his worth proclaim,
And wreath with greatful memories
    His loved and honoured name.

Comforted.

--

ALONE, alone, e'en in the midſt,
  Of yonder glittering throng;
Where every lip bore Pleaſure's ſmile,
  And every voice her ſong:
Tho' youth was her's, and all her path
  With gems, and flowers ſeemed bright,
And ſhe upon the ſhining way,
  Shone as a peerleſs light.

Young, rich, and beautiful, and yet
  The world's gay thoughtleſs round
Of wit and mirth, bore to her heart
  A weary, empty found;
One voice was huſhed, one heart was cold,
  One dear loved ſmile was gone,
And all the reſt ſeemed nothingneſs—
  Alas! ſhe was alone.

Where might she flee? where find the rest
　　Her young heart fought in vain?
Where nurse the grief, which now must shroud
　　All future years in pain?
That memory of him so loved,
　　So loving, and so brave,
Sleeping beneath a far-off sky,
　　Within a soldier's grave.

O should she, wandering 'neath the shade
　　Of her anceftral trees,
Find comfort in the tears, and sighs
　　Breathed on each pasling breeze;
Or loving sun, and silent stars,
　　And gentle silvery moon,
Only because their light was shed
　　Upon that far-off tomb!

Not so! those same bright sun and stars,
　　Brought to her drooping heart,
Some thoughts of Him who bade them shine,
　　And gave to each his part

Of light, and labour in the world,
   Nor had withheld her own,
Henceforth fhe too would venture forth,
   Nor mourn fhe was alone.

And He who ruled the waters wild,
   And bade the tempeft ceafe,
Looked down upon His weary child,
   And foftly whifpered "Peace:"
Taught her to find in life's dark ways,
   Grief deeper than her own,
And learn to feel in healing it,
   She need not be alone.

And fo her youthful years went by,
   When o'er our ftartled land,
Came tales of forrow from afar,
   Tales of our hero-band,
Who went to battle for th' oppreffed
   On the Crimean plains,
Dying in bitter cold, neglect,
   With none to foothe their pains.

Thither she went, where men's strong hearts
    Had sickened, shrunk, and quailed,
Her woman's spirit fainted not,
    Her woman's heart ne'er failed :
Within Scutari's 'leagured walls,
    Where victims of the war
Lay stretched in life's last agony
    From Home, and friends afar.

What wonder that to them she seemed
    An angel from above,
Whose white hands smoothed their dying beds—
    Whose lips breathed words of love ;
Who pointed up to Heav'n their eyes
    And bade them learn in death,
To bear their pain unmurmuring,
    And peaceful yield their breath.

What wonder, too, that brightest far
    All other names beside,
We English women count her name
    Most worthy of our pride ;

And write for her—whofe heart leaped up—
   At fuch a noble call,
" Many have wifely done, and well,
   But *thou* excelleft *all.*"

Wrecked !

In a lonely corner of the quiet churchyard of the once fecluded, but now popular watering-place of Walton-on-the-Naze, apart from other graves, may be feen a fmall monumental stone—*namelefs*; but bearing the word "MISERARE," with two appropriate texts. This was erected by fubfcription among fome of the vifitors who were enjoying the fea-breezes in that locality during the fummer of 1856, and whofe fympathies were aroufed by the fad incident which the following lines will tell :—

POOR broken heart! above thy grave,
　　Unhonoured and unknown,
Shall no relentlefs words be breathed,
　　No ftern rebukings come ;
But tears of pity fhed their dew
　　Upon that namelefs grave,
Whofe only requiem has been,
　　The wailing of the wave.

No heart can tell the agony
　　Thy quivering fpirit bore,
Ere its fierce madnefs drove thee on
　　To feek th' eternal fhore,

And filenced e'en the Mother's voice
　　In thy grief-ftricken breaft,
Or, for thy Babe thou might'ft have lived,
　　And left to God the reft.

Oh! that fome voice of love had breathed,
　　In that laft dreadful hour,
And poured into thy weary heart
　　The balm of healing power,—
Had told of Hope, and Peace, and Heaven,
　　And fnatched thee from thy fate,—
For there was even peace for *thee*,
　　Tho' more than defolate.

We weep for thee, unhappy child
　　Of forrow and of fhame,
Thy Beauty's fun, gone down for aye,
　　Behind a clouded name;
But moft we weep the wafted wealth
　　Of Woman's faith and truft,
The treafure of affection poured
　　To mingle with the duft.

But there is one, upon whofe heart
  A weary weight will dwell,
And in whofe ears, through life, fhall ring
  The echo of thy knell,—
In brighteft fcenes and happieft hours,
  A gloomy fhade fhall fall,
(Tho' faireft flowers his path may ftrew,)
  Dark as funereal pall.

The afhes of thy blafted peace
  Shall rife in forms of ftrife,
And dafh with bittereft memories
  His fweeteft cup of life.
Though far away may be his home
  The voices of the fea
Shall haunt his dreams with one fad fong—
  The memory of THEE.

The Passing Crowd.

IT surges on—sweeps past my gazing eye,
    I, but an unit on the billows borne,
Of this great torrent of humanity,
    Amid its thousands, friendless, and alone.

On with the busy crowd, yet as I go,
    With curious interest I strive to trace,
Some glimpses of the hidden heart and life,
    Written upon each silent unknown face.

Here youth's bright eyes and fair unfurrowed brow,
    Tell their own tale of Hope! and light within,
Undimmed as yet by touch of pain or care,
    Unmarred by the yet deeper stain of sin.

Hard faces meet me—stern-set, brooding brow,
    With lines of Beauty long since clouded o'er,
And lips compressed with weight of anxious care,
    As if the smile might never part them more.

Here fweeps along—kid-gloved Profperity,
 In fpecklefs broad-cloth, or in filken fheen,
While Poverty in Rags, cold, gaunt, and pale,
 In miferable contraft fteps between.

And fo it rolls, this mighty tide of life,
 Each by a feparate impulfe fwept along,
Each heart's own purpofes, and cares, and joys,
 Borne filently, and veilèd from the throng.

Whither, or to what goal each footftep bends
 In Joy, or Sorrow, that I may not know,
Some o'er Life's flowery ways of pleafant eafe,
 Some o'er the thorny path of Want and Woe.

Nought to the Multitude; yet each a part
 Of fome loved circle where they reign fupreme,
Each dear and beautiful to fome fond heart,
  Where tears, and fmiles may find their anfwering
  gleam.

And each one guided on the bufy way,
 Watched over by the fame unfleeping eye,
Cared for by One—The One who bade them live,
 And traced each path beneath his own broad fky.

City Graves.

—

LITTLE to thee—perchance thefe plots
  Of homely burial ground,
Lefs to the bufy world of wealth,
  Which circle them around,
Yet *all* to fome, within whofe hearts,
  Long will the memory ftay
Of tender love which bleft them once
  For ever paft away.

No marble pomp may crown the place,
  No bloffoms deck the foil,
Where peaceful reft 'mid London's ftrife
  Her fons of want and toil;
Yet are they fpots of hallowed ground,
  By every tear-drop fhed,
By all the anguifh which embalms,
  The Memory of the Dead.

Then let the fleepers reft, while yet
    Affection's foot may come,
And willful paufe in tender love,
    Befide their laft long home.
While yet thofe eyes which wept fo long,
    Their yearning gaze may turn,
Where fank the fun-light of their lives
    To never more return.

To ev'ry name which love has traced,
    Above the burial fpot,
The fweep of Time and Change fhall come,
    And write its doom " Forgot."
Yet for awhile let reverent hands
    The fpoiler's tafk delay,
At leaft till thofe who loved them once,
    Shall all have paft away.

City Trees.

———

BRIGHT TREES! ye're always beautiful,
  Dreffed in your living green,
Flinging your pleafant fhadows down,
  With funlit fpots between.
By homes that neftle in your fhade,
  O'er landfcapes fmiling fair,
O precious gifts, ye fhine, and wave
  A bleffing everywhere.

But here a tenfold charm ye have,
  Here, in the throbbing heart
Of London; claiming even there
  For nature ftill a part,
And flinging o'er the bufy way
  Where rolls that mighty tide
Of eager, reftlefs human life,
  Some pleafant thought befide.

For though some eyes may be too dim,
　　Some hearts too hard, or cold,
To mark your beauty where ye shed
　　Your glorious green and gold.
To many another weary one
　　That beauty shining fair
May bring some hopes of happy things—
　　Some little rest from care.

The stranger, lonely 'midst the throng,
　　Afar from friends and home,
May catch a glimpse of leaf and bough,
　　And feel not quite alone.
His fainting heart bowed down beneath
　　A weight of anxious fear,
May courage take, and seeing you
　　Feel that God too is here.

Then spare the City Trees—ye men
　　Whose eager footsteps press,
To span with works of giant might
　　This crowded wilderness.

No voice here fpeaks to ftay the courfe
　　Of Great Improvement's plan,
But when ye fee a pleafant tree,
　　Oh! fpare it, if ye can.

The Poor Man to his Richer Brother,

After a long Seafon of Diftrefs in the Winter of 1861 ·2.

THANK GOD! 'tis paft—the bitter hour
    Of keeneft want and woe.
How bitter only thofe can tell
    Who the fierce cravings know
Of Poverty in *all* its pain—
    Food, light, and warmth denied;
When other men, more fortunate,
    Enjoy their fnug firefide.

Ye felt the blaft whofe icy breath
    Bound as with iron bands
Alike the currents and the foil,
    And ftopped the willing hands,
Which elfe in honeft toil had wrought
    To earn their daily bread,
And keep the fhelter of a roof
    Above each weary head.

Ye felt it, tho' well clad and filled,
　　Soft laid, and warmly housed.
Pain,—almost death it seemed to us,
　　Which but your slumber roused.
O, did your thankful hearts then turn
　　To help a brother's need?
And open wide a generous hand
　　The helpless ones to feed?

Ye did, and may a blessing rest—
　　The blessing of the Poor—
Upon each kindly heart who gave,
　　From its more liberal store;
That charity, whose rich full streams,
　　Unchecked, have thus been poured,
In the dark hour of bitter need,
　　God surely will reward.

If there's a bond 'twixt man and man
　　More noble and more good
Than all the rest, 'tis, when close linked
　　In Holy Brotherhood,

They look abroad, and feek to fhed
    A little gleam of light
Upon the path which elfe would be
    Black, piercing, ftarlefs night.

And if a recompenfe is gained
    Sweeter than all the reft,
It waits upon that toil of love
    Which, *bleffing*, fhall be bleft ;
There flows acrofs the large, warm heart
    Which felt a Brother's woes—
A deep, full tide of happinefs
    That nothing elfe beftows.

America in the midst of War.

———

AMERICA! thou Sister-land
   Bound by no common ties
To Britiſh hearts who link thy name
   With ſacred memories;
We cannot watch with careleſs eyes
   Or ſtand indifferent by
While throbs thine heart's core in the throes
   Of War's great agony.

And yet, 'tis not for North or South
   We, looking from afar,
Can take the part. We only pray
   One iſſue from this war:
And that, thou glorious Weſtern World
   So proudly called "The Free,"
O'er all thy vaſt expanſe may know
   The truth of Liberty.

We watch and pray, that through thy land
    The ſtrife of blood may ceaſe,
That once again ſerene ſhall riſe
    The Holy Star of Peace.
That, where thy ſwords are laid to reſt
    Within a blood-ſtained grave,
There, too, may lie as uſeleſs things
    The fetters of the Slave!

For we remember 'twas thy ſoil
    Our Pilgrim Fathers trod
When firſt they wandered forth to find
    Freedom, to worſhip God.
For ever muſt their memory
    Unite our ſouls to thee,
And by that memory we pray
    Thou may'ſt again be free.

O North! with all thy wealth and ſtrength,
    Can nothing now eraſe
This fierce and bitter ſtrife which burns
    In boſoms of one race?

O South! with all thine ancient love
    Of noble chivalry,
Can'ft thou not take thy brother's hand
    And fling thy weapons by?

Not grafping take, not craven yield,
    But each in forrow meet
To own ye've much to be forgiven,
    And each much to forget.
Then, from thy ftormy night may rife
    A brighter, clearer day,
And its fair dawn behold thy *curse*
    Of Slavery fwept away.

Poland in 1862-3.

——

THE years which brought to other lands
  New hopes, new liberty,
Have darkly broken on thy fhores,
  And borne no joys for thee.
Poor Poland! yet no falt'ring hands,
  No craven hearts were thine,
'Midft thofe who've learned to bear and wait
  Until th' appointed time—

The time when all thy fons might rife
  Bound in one brotherhood,
To win the freedom of their foil
  E'en with their heart's life-blood.
And lo, 'tis come! the burning wrongs
  Long ftern and filent borne,
The pent-up paffion breaks at length—
  One fierce and mighty ftorm.

One common vengeance fires each heart,
    One hope burns in each breast,
To break the Muscovite's stern yoke,
    And trust God for the rest.
No thirst of conquest or of gain
    Has borne them thro' this strife,
Who only ask—our human right—
    Sweet Liberty! dear life!

But courage, Poland! that deep wail
    Wrung from thy heart's despair,
Has thrill'd earth's nations and awoke
    Responsive echoes there.
They watch'd thy throes with bated breath:
    Oh! could they bear to see
Thee fall, when one strong helping arm
    Had made thee blest and free?

But thou hast hoped and waited long,
    And in thy night of woe—
Pale—weary-eyed thou wanderest forth
    Thy bitterest fate to know,

And on the heart of Europe laid
　　Thy hand in trembling queſt—
To find it pulſeleſs, cold and ſtill
　　For all thou loveſt beſt.

Then ſadly turned thee back to ſeek
　　Thy deſolated throne
To bravely ſtrive and ſuffer ſtill
　　Unaided and alone.
Alas! 'tis now a martyr's crown
　　That ſhines upon thy brow,
And God, who ſee'ſt all thy pain,
　　Alone can help thee now.

The Cry from Circassia.

In the summer of 1861, there came to our shores two delegates from Circaffia to reprefent to our Government the haplefs condition of their native land, then refifting to the utmoft the tyranny of Ruffia. They were alfo the bearers of a petition to our Queen, couched in the moft pathetic fimplicity, that fome meafures (not warlike, but merely remonftrative) might be taken by England to check that cruel aggreffion. The forrowful conclufion of the ftruggle is known to all, but the following poem is a paraphrafe of their touching petition, which may not be fo generally known.

O BROTHERS of the fair, free land,
    On the far weftern wave,
In this our hour of fad defpair,
    We afk your power to fave.
For o'er the diftant land and fea,
    To our wild mountain home,
A tower of ftrength, a ftar of hope,
    Your name and fame have come.
The ftory of your noble deeds
    For liberty and right,
Has bade our fad defpairing hearts,
    Yet look for joy's fweet light.

Long years have fped fince peace or joy
　　Have fmiled upon our land—
For many years we have fought and bled,
　　To ſtay the oppreffor's hand—
The graſping power which fain would bind
　　Our free limbs, with her chain ;
And wipe from out the nations roll,
　　Circaffia's ſtainleſs name.
Oh, muſt it be that thus for aye,
　　Our out-poured blood and tears,
Muſt fail to fave the homes we've held,
　　For full five thouſand years ?
Why muſt we fee our manhood's prime,
　　Our fair youth's golden life,
For ever waſted in the throes,
　　Of this unequal ſtrife ?
While other lands rejoicing, reap
　　The treaſures of their foil,
We dare not ſtay to taſte the ſweets,
　　Of reſt or honeſt toil.
Yet from the Caſpian's filver tide,
　　To Euxine's flowery ſhores,
The land we yet can call our own,
　　Is rich in golden ſtores;

And Elbrou's mighty fteep looks down
  Upon a fcenc as fair,
As though no deeds of bloody ftrife,
  Were daily acted there.
O England, not your wealth, or blood,
  But your all-powerful word
We afk, to bid our forrows ceafe,
  And fheath the defpot's fword.
Give this, and we are free; wiped out
  Our agonies, our tears:
And in our joy, we may forget
  The woes of fifty years.

1864.

Two fummers' funs have fhed their glow,
  O'er Englifh hearths and homes,
Since, o'er the land this laft fad wail
  Breathed out its mournful tones.
To us, two years of hope, and peace,
  But what can now be faid
Of thofe brave, patient, fuffering hearts,
  Whofe laft faint hope is dead.
We heard—but heeded not—and they
  Far from their own loved land,

Faint, fall, and die—cruſhed out at laſt
  By Ruſſia's ruthleſs hand.
Too late—O England, e'en for thee
  To help, or ſave them now ;
Yet Ruſſia with her blood-ſtained hands,
  Is *scarce more wrong* than thou.
But haply, tho' it ſeem in vain
  Thy late repentance comes ;
Though thou can'ſt never build again
  Thoſe outraged mountain homes;
Some kindly ſympathy of thine
  May ſoft, and gently fall,
Once, it was granted thee *to help*,
  But *now, this* is thy *all.*

Italy and its Liberator.

O ITALY! beautiful Slave of the South,
How long haſt thou languiſhed 'neath tyranny's ſway,
But now may'ſt thou raiſe thy fair neck from the duſt,
And hail the bright dawning of Liberty's day!

Thy olive-trees bloomed, and thy Poet-ſons ſang.
And the wealth of thy genius went forth o'er the
earth:
And the ſtranger-land reaped the rich fruits of thy
ſtore,
While bleeding and cruſhed lay the land of their
birth.

'Thy Beauty was aſhes! Thy garlands were hung
O'er a charnel-houſe foul with deep wrongs, and deep
woe.
Where a thouſand brave hearts of thy nobleſt and beſt
Have groaned forth the anguiſh no mortal may know.

But the voice of thy groaning kind Heaven has heard,
　　And has nerved the brave heart of thy lowly-born Son
To fight the hard conflict of Right againſt Might,
　　And he lays at thy feet the bright crown he has won!

No dreams of Ambition have ſtirred that brave heart:—
　　GARIBALDI! for Freedom alone haſt thou ſtriven;
And lo! thou haſt triumphed—the land thou haſt ſaved
　　In deep gratitude lifts up a free voice to Heaven.

And we of the Iſle on the far weſtern wave,
　　Tho' ſtrangers to all but thy world-echoed Name,
Would prefs thy rough hand in a brother's warm claſp—
　　Rejoice in thy triumph and honour thy fame!

For truly our hearts have gone forth on thy path:
　　Tho' in this our free England we never may know
The deep wrongs that have ſtirred thee to do and to dare,
　　And ſtrike the foul Upas-tree down at a blow!

Thou wert noble in triumph—O nobler far, now!
　　In thine iſlet of peace calmly caſting aſide
The ſnares which have dazzled Rome's great ones of yore,
　　Till they ſtumbled and fell in the hour of their pride;

There was a moment of forrow and anguifh,
 Thy brave heart half-broken by falfehood and wrong;
But time hath brought balm and hath taught us the
  leffon—
 By the pain of her heroes doth freedom grow ftrong.

Yet mayft thou triumph! thy life's noble purpofe
 Muft fee its fruition. The work is not done,
Till the Queen of the Sea, and the Seven-hilled City—
 Fair Venice, and Rome, are for Italy won.

Anita.

—

A BRIDAL MORN; but ufhered in
  By no fuperb array ;
No peal of bells, no fumptuous feaft
  Proclaimed her wedding day.
No gleam of pearl, or filken fheen
  Shone o'er that fair young bride,
Who ftood in holy faith that day,
    By Garibaldi's fide.

Yet ne'er were bridal vows breathed forth,
  From heart more nobly true ;
No deeper love was ever won,
  Than that Anita knew.
The ardent zeal which filled his breaft,
  Flafhed in her earneft eye ;
Ready with him in Freedom's caufe
    To conquer, or to die.

Straight from the altar to the fight,
  With heart that never quailed ;
While round her fell the rain of death,
  She fainted not, nor failed.
This was her bridal ; fitting type
  Of all her after-life ;
Where'er the fearlefs hufband went
  There went his fearlefs wife.

At laft ! the life of faithful love
  Sank in a lonely grave—
She fleeps beneath the fouthern fky,
  Befide the fouthern wave ;
And woe! for him to wander forth,
  And tread the world alone ;
Whatever time might keep in ftore,
  It feemed that love was gone.

Yet 'tis not fo,—the babe whofe fmile
  Had made their ftruggles fweet, —
Drew with his life the fame true foul
  That in her bofom beat.

G 2

Menotti ſtands, a living ſhield
By his brave father's ſide ;
Love had not faded from his life
Although Anita died.

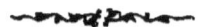

Aspromonte.

———

"ROME OR DEATH!" the cry thrilled forth
 Upon the startled air—
Not shouted in defiant tones,
 But in imploring prayer.
While through the Autumn's clustering vines
 A Patriot-band passed by;
Their Southern natures all aglow,
 Their bosoms beating high.

For once, again, their Chieftain's voice
 Had called them from afar—
Once more their Chieftain's flag unfurled,
 Italia Unita!
And "ROME OR DEATH!" Marsala heard
 And echoed forth the cry;
Palermo's thousands thrilled to see
 The far-off hope drawn nigh:

" Romo-o-Morte!" Catania's voice
   The midnight filence broke—
As with one ftart, and with one voice
   The fleeping City woke.
And oh! for that great noble heart,
   Could *less* than Rome fuffice?
The hope of all thofe patient years
   Of toil and facrifice!

O, but to free their country's hands
   From odious foreign chain,
And fee the crown of ancient days
   Upon her brow again!
So through the fragrant myrtle bowers
   They fped their hopeful way;
Their morrow brightened with the glow
   That lit their yefterday.

There was a waking from that dream,
   That funlight fank in fhade;
They went to ftrive for Italy—
   But Italy betrayed!

So Aspromonte! 'twas for thee
  To hear the parting knell
Of trust in kingly gratitude
  When Garibaldi fell!

He fell—and long death hovered o'er
  His prison-couch of pain,
But God in mercy brought him back
  To life and hope again.
And now, O Country, twice enriched,
  He still exists for thee--
Not "ROME OR DEATH," but "ROME AND LIFE,"
  To win for Italy.

A Welcome to Garibaldi.

CROWNED kings and mighty potentates
　　Have fought our island shore,
Laden with gifts of gems and gold
　　To add unto our store.
To many a noble one we've given
　　A welcome full and free,
But none more earnest or more true
　　Than that which waits for thee.
Hero and Patriot, loved by all
　　Who only know thy name,
Which o'er a slowly waking world
　　In startling magic came,
Coupled with deeds so great, and rare
　　That, when their tale was told,
It seemed as we had turned to read
　　Some wondrous page of old.

Uncrowned and fceptrelefs thou comeft,
  Yet not the lefs a king,
Whofe honoured name, o'er hiftory's page,
  A glorious light fhall fling
Great as Leonidas of old,
  And yet a greater one
Than Rienzi—Rome's patriot fon,
  And laft ill-ftarred tribune.
Though the long years we fadly gazed
  O'er thofe fair claffic plains,
And palace-crefted hills which lay
  Crufhed in the tyrant's chains ;
That land of funfhine, flowers, and fong,
  The home of tears and gloom,
Beneath whofe cloudlefs Heaven ftood
  St. Elmo's living tomb.
We fighed and waited, 'till at length,
  Triumphant o'er her foes,
Strong-nerved, thy Italy to fave,
  Thou, GARIBALDI, rofe.
And England's heart went with thee then
  Upon thy conquering way—
The fame great heart which proudly bids
  Thee welcome here to-day.

It is alone that thou haſt trod
  Italia's ſlavedom down,
Nor that ſuch ſtirring memories wreath
  About thy laurel crown—
Of royal Naples won to life,
  Of Capua free once more,
Vareſe unbound, and Freedom's ſong
  By Como's lovely ſhore.
Nor leſs thoſe Aſpromontine plains
  Stained with the martyr blood
Of one who only ſought to work
  An ingrate country's good.
We welcome thee, and honour thee,
  Moſt for that loyal heart,
Whoſe high ambition could afford
  To ſet itſelf apart,
And let the crown and ſceptre paſs,
  As glittering baubles by,
Whilſt thou, unbought, content, and poor,
  Still liv'ſt for liberty.

Farewell to Garibaldi.

———

FAREWELL! We fpeak the parting words
   Reluctant, fad, and flow,
And feel, with bofoms ftrangely ftirred,
   We fcarce can let thee go.
We fain had held thee longer here,
   Moft loved, moft honoured gueft;
But, trufting thee, we ftrive to feel
   E'en this is for the beft.

To welcome thee, our palace gates
   Were widely open flung!
To welcome thee, our teeming throngs
   Thy name in rapture fung!
And Garibaldi, in *thy* heart
   We know will be enfhrined
Fond memories of the Englifh fhores
   Thou leaveft far behind.

Once, *but a name* upon our lips:
　　We hail thee *Brother* now:
We've grafped thy hand, we've gazed upon
　　Thy grave and kindly brow.
Thy pleafant prefence in our midft—
　　Thy fmile—thy earneft tone—
Are memories that will keep their charm
　　For many a year to come.

Thou'rt gone! But *now* new power fhall gild
　　The preftige of thy name:
A new-born ftrength of heart and arm
　　Shall nerve thee in thine aim
When on thy conquering march to win
　　All that is good and free!
Thou knoweft—and the world, too, knows—
　　That England is with thee.

Then, fare-thee-well, Gueft—Brother—Friend!
　　The leffening fail which bears
Thee to thy lone and fea-girt home
　　Is freighted with our prayers,

Our fympathy, our love, our hopes,
That thou wilt ftrength regain,
And in fome brighter, happier days,
Come to our land again.

To His Royal Highness the Prince of Wales.

———

As from a ſtarleſs night of gloom
    Breaks forth the joyful day,
Whoſe golden hues of new-born light
    Chaſe all the clouds away ;
So, merging from its clouds of grief,
    The Nation hails the dawn,
And greets with joy, Young Prince of Wales,
    Thy happy Wedding Morn.

Hark ! o'er the land ten thouſand ſpires
    Peal forth their glad acclaim,
And every Engliſh heart invokes
    A bleſſing on thy name ;
And prays for life-long happineſs
    For thee and thy fair Bride,
Whoſe love may bring thee greater joy
    Than all thy wealth beſide.

Whofe young life holds thy Truth, thy Faith,
  Thine heart's-love all her own;
Gems of a luftre brighter far
  Than even England's crown;
And counts the privilege more dear
  To fhare a happy home,
Than all the glitter of a Court,
  Or glory of a Throne.

Born to Earth's nobleft heritage,
  Our Hope, our Pride, our Heir;
The " triple plume " ne'er waved above
  A princely path more fair.
No longer 'mid the battle borne,
  A Victor's flaming creft,
In Peace its ancient glory fhines,
  With ten-fold luftre bleft.

God fend thee ever Peace and Joy—
  Peace in thy palace-home;
Peace over all thy broad fair realm
  That hails thee as her own.

May our lov'd Albert's wife, pure life,
   In thine reflected be,
That Queen and People both may feel
   He lives again in thee.

England's Welcome to Her Royal Highness the Princess Alexandra of Denmark, our future Queen.

— —

ALEXANDRA! from thy northern home,
   Acrofs the ftormy fea,
To our fair Ifland of the Weft,
   In joy, we welcome thee.

Our cannons boom, our banners wave,
   Joy-bells from fpire and dome,
And earneft voices, welcome thee
   To thine adopted home.

Our garlands wave their wreaths of bloom,
   Bright o'er thy fair young head;
And maidens ftrew the path with flowers
   Where firft thy feet fhall tread;

And, with our glittering array
   Of ancient pomp and pride,
We hail thee, Daughter of the Land,
   Our Prince's chofen Bride!

H

Though still perhaps thine heart may ache
    With pain of parting tears,
Shed o'er thy Fatherland and home
    Of all thy happy years.

Yet weep not. Maiden never won
    A brighter destiny
Of princely wealth and regal power
    Than that which waits for thee;

But more than these: a happier lot
    Than crown or throne might prove:
Thou comest to share, with Albion's heir,
    A Home of Peace and Love!

And, many-voiced, the nation prays
    That sky which looks so fair,
May ne'er for thee be shaded o'er
    With clouds of grief or care.

But long, long years of happy life
    To thee and thine be given;
Bright earnest of a brighter one
    Which waits for thee in Heaven.

Address to our beloved Queen on the Marriage of the Prince of Wales.

— — —

DEAR Sovereign Lady of our Land,
　So lov'd through happy years,
And held in deeper reverence,
　In sorrow and in tears;
The people of thy gentle sway,
　In tender silence stood;
Whilst o'er thee swept the first dark waves
　Of thy sad Widowhood.

We wept, and ever weep with thee
　By thy lov'd Albert's tomb,
Whose life so wise, so pure, so great,
　Was quenched in Death so soon;
As we have grieved, so in this hour
　Of deep and chastened joy,
We gently at thy feet would lay
　A Nation's sympathy.

H 2

O may thine heart be glad once more,
　　May children's loving care
Pierce through the clouds which fhroud its joy
　　And paint a rainbow there;
We pray that new-born hopes and joys
　　Thy future years may blefs,
And bid that tender heart awake
　　Anew to happinefs.

May He who watches o'er thy path
　　His heavenly peace fend down,
And grant the current of thy life
　　May tranquilly glide on;
And that pure fhrine of houfehold love,
　　Blefs'd by His gracious hand,
Still fhed its hallowed influence
　　O'er our well favor'd land!

In Memory of Mrs. Mary Wood, Chicago, America.

In Memory; in memory of one
    Who walked Life's journey as 'tis feldom trod,
Bright witnefs of the Faith which ruled her life
    And made it beautiful, to man and God.
A life of gentleft charity, and love
    Shedding far round the luftre of its rays
Whofe calm confiftency and holy truth
    Graced her fair youth, and crowned her lateft days.

In loving memory of her whofe love
    Made her far home a place of peacful reft
Through all life's ftorms, in every grief and care,
    To thofe who 'neath her influence were bleft.
Wife, mother, fifter, friend, in all
    Life's fweet relationfhips, fhe filled her part
Perfect before His fight, who only knows
    The inmoft workings of His creature's heart.

In forrowing memory of her who fleeps
  In her far grave, acrofs th' Atlantic fea,
Whofe voice and fmile may never more rejoice
  The heart who treafured her dear memory,
Mourning; yet not as others mourn; for fhe
  In joy has entered her eternal reft,
In the fair land where grief may never come,
  Happy for ever, and for ever bleft.

"Not Dead, but Gone Before."

DEAR LITTLE ADA: ah! how foon
  The golden links were riven;
How foon thou'ft winged thine angel-flight
  Back to thy native heaven.

Thy parents weep; ah, could their care
  Have kept thee by their fide,
Or tendereft love availed thee aught,
  Thou, darling, had'ft not died.

They loved thee, but 'twas thine to know
  An even greater love,
E'en His who took thee from their arms
  To dwell with Him above.

Took thee in earlieft morning hours
  While thy fair infant life
Scarce ftained by fin, unknown to woe
  Paffed from a world of ftrife.

Dear cherifhed one ; how hard it feemed,
   To lay thee down fo foon ;
And feel how many happy hopes
   Lie broken in thy tomb.

But it is beft ; for who can tell
   What weight of grief or care,
If to thy life long years had come,
   Thou might'ft have had to bear ?

Thy tiny grave, beneath the trees,
   May call forth bitter tears,
And pierce with many a forrow-pang
   The joy of future years.

But thou art bleft, at reft for aye,
   Free from all grief and pain ;
And thou fhalt lead their hearts to where
   Ye all fhall meet again.

Consolation.

O MOTHER! e'en in this fad hour
   Of deep, and bitter Grief,
Be comforted, for He who fmites,
   Doth alfo fend relief.
Be comforted, tho' in thy pain,
   The joy Exiftence gave,
Seems buried where thy dear one fleeps
   Within her early grave.

For many a Mother, weeping, too,
   For a beloved One gone,
May have no anchor, fuch as thine,
   In ftorms to reft upon.
No Faith like thine whofe eye can fee,
   Beyond the filent grave,
The Glory of the Life He gives,
   Who gave His own to fave.

And many paſſing through the Shade,
  Like her in Life's bright Youth,
Have paſſed beneath the awful porch,
  Unknowing Hope, or Truth.
Or Faith like hers, whoſe mighty power,
  Bridged o'er the gulf of Death,
And bade her ſing of Peace, and Heaven
  E'en with her lateſt breath.

'Tis hard to leave her cold, and lone,
  The neſtling of thy breaſt,
But ſweet to think of her above,
  Safe, happy, and at reſt.
'Tis hard to feel her loving voice,
  From hence has ever gone,
But ſweet to think that voice is raiſed
  In praiſe before the Throne.

She paſſed in brighteſt morning hours,
  E're ſhade of doubt or care
Had touched her heart—but who knows what
  Years might have brought to bear?

'Tis well: The Hand who gave Thy child,
  Sent e'en this ſtroke in love,
The bud ye miſs ſo ſore at home
  Is ſafer far above.

To the Queen, on the Death of her late Royal Highness the Duchess of Kent.

———

ROYAL LADY ! while thou weepest forth
   Thine heart's great weight of grief,
In this sad hour when all thy state
   Can bring thee no relief—
The People of thy gentle rule
   Stand hushed and silent by ;
And softly at thy feet would lay
   A nation's sympathy.

As in thy golden hours of joy,
   We, too, have gladdened been ;
And gloried in the happiness
   Of our Beloved Queen—
So do we mourn o'er that first shade
   Which on thy path is shed ;
And tenderly would weep with thee
   O'er that Beloved Dead.

And many-voiced, in earneft tones,
    A Nation's prayers afcend,
That thou wilt heavenly comfort gain
    From HIM, the Mourner's Friend ;
And e'en rejoice fo fair a life
    Such peace in death has won,
And everlafting blifs been gained
    For thy departed one.

The tendereft memories will fling
    A halo round her name,
Whofe gentle wifdom led thy youth,
    And bleffed thy happy reign.
And now a brighter diadem
    Than ever monarch wore,
Graces her brow, in that bleft Land
    Where pain fhall be no more!

A Nation's Wail on the Death of Albert, the Consort of the Queen.

— ——

O DARK is the shadow, and bitter the sorrow,
 Which wide o'er the breadth of our Country is
  spread :
Loud and deep is the cry of her great lamentation—
 The voice of a Nation bewailing her dead !

Death has entered the Palace—fulfilled his dread miffion;
 Defolation fits brooding in that Royal Home,
Where late the pure joys of domeftic affection
 Eclipfed e'en the fplendour which circled the Throne.

O well may ye weep—Sons and Daughters of England !
 O'er the Prefence departed which lately did fhine
As the nobleft of Princes, the pride of the Nation,
 Paffed away in the glory of Manhood's fair prime.

The grey Caftle ftands in its old regal grandeur,
 Holds ftill the cold glitter of fceptre and fway—
But all that remains of its dearly loved Mafter,
 Is a cold, fhrouded form of infenfible clay !

Mourn!—not for him—since the God who has
    smitten
  Knoweth beft His own time; and "His great will
    done;"
Since we dare to believe that the loved Prince
    departed
  Has exchanged Earth's poor ftate for a far brighter
    home!

But weep for our Sovereign, for her Children thus
    ftricken;
  Overwhelmed in the anguifh of this mighty grief.
Alas for fuch forrow!—*One* only can foothe it—
  May He look on the Mourners, and fend them relief!

Poor Queen!—written "*Widow*"—so late bleft and
    happy!
  Lefs our pride as a Monarch, than Mother and Wife;
We mingle our tears o'er the Grave where has faded
  For ever, the love-light which gladdened thy life.

Beloved of thy people—twice dear in thy forrow!
  Every heart fhares thy grief, every lip breathes a
    prayer:
God comfort and blefs thee, till, in His own feafon,
  He calls thee, the blifs of thy loft one to fhare.

The Children's Appeal.

"ONLY THE LITTLE ONES," you fay,
  "Stopping us on our bufy way—
Small pleadings—pafs them by."
  Ah! ye the rich and well-to-do,
With Children bleft, and happy too,
  Lift to our lowly cry.

We, Children of the fuffering Poor,
  Your kind and generous help implore
To raife a Sunday School,
  Where we may learn Truth's pleafant ways,
Be taught to know in early days
  Religion's gentle rule.

Our lives are hard; alas! 'tis ours
  To gather more of thorns than flowers
Along the rugged road;
  But ye may blefs our lowly lot,
Teach us to bear, and murmur not,
  And lift our hearts to God.

O tender hearts ! by all the love
   Upon your own beſtowed—
By all your bleſſings given —
   Let us too learn of higher life,
Of ſtrength to meet the world's fierce ſtrife,
   Of peace and reſt in Heaven.

The City Hospital.

—

GIVE, GIVE! how oft the hungry call
   Has fallen on your ear,
Burthened with many a plaintive figh,
   And many a falling tear;
So oft, perchance, that in thy heart
   The funny, loving ray
Of Charity—fweet Charity—
   Hath almoft died away.

Yet here it comes, with greater force;
   O clofe not heart and hand,
But, by the nobleft impulfe led,
   Bid thy whole foul expand—
Expand, and melt; that fick, and fad,
   And fuffering ones may find
By thy free, generous, gracious aid
   That "Charity is kind."

Though now the tide of life and health
  Glides calmly through each vein,
Clear brains to think, ftrong arms to work,
  And fcarce a thought of pain;
Yet think thee of thofe days gone by
  When life was not fo fair,
When pain and ficknefs made that life
  A burden hard to bear.

When by thy couch of languifhing,
  The tendereft care and love
Spent all their power of gentlenefs,
  Yet often failed to foothe,
Till the Great Healer's gracious hand
  Rolled back the tide of pain,
And gave once more the precious gifts
  Of health and ftrength again.

In grateful memory of that time
  Your willing offerings bring
For thofe who fuffer all the pain
  With Want's fharp, added fting.

But who may find the help they need
  In thefe wide-opened doors,
If only Charity will give
  Some of her bleffed ftores.

A Plea for Ragged Schools.

STAY: ye who tread life's pleasant ways,
  Whose path lies through the flowers;
Bright skies o'er head, and scarce a cloud
  To shade the summer hours.
It may be, in your favored lot
  Not many thoughts arise
Of that great misery which lives
  Beneath the same bright skies,
Which round your path, within your reach,
  Drags out its weary life
Of craving want, and gaunt despair,
  And sin's unholy strife;
Not many thoughts (while round your knees
  Your little children press,
And warm your heart with sunny smile
  And innocent caress,)
Of childhood in another guise,
  Bereaven of its grace,
Shorn in the sorrow of its birth
  Of every pleasant trace.

Yet fuch there are, but o'er their fate,
  There dawns a glimmering ray,
Which, with God's help, at length may break
  Into meridian day.
Bleffings on thofe who've lent their zeal
  To feed, to teach, reclaim,
And lead thefe " Arabs of the ftreet "
  To win a better name.
To find that they may fhare the gifts
  God's gracious hands fend down—
For them the recompenfe of toil—
  For them a heavenly crown.
Workers for good : O may ye find
  Rich harveft for your toil,
Fair flowers, and fruits to fpring to life
  E'en from this barren foil.
Still from the blacknefs of their lot
  Bright gems may fparkling fhine ;
Still from the darknefs may break forth
  The latent fpark divine,
Which kindling 'neath the influence
  Of gentle, guiding hand,
May make our Ragged Schools to be
  The bleffing of the land.

The Power of Small Things.

As drop by drop, the ocean vaſt
  Swelled 'neath its Maker's hand ;
As grain by grain, the mighty hills
  Roſe o'er the pleaſant land ;

As leaf by leaf, and bud by bud,
  And blade by blade unfurled,
A myriad tiny things make up
  The beauty of a world.

And as the works of human ſkill,
  The pride of many a land,
The palace dome, the giant bridge
  Have, ſtone by ſtone, been ſpanned ;

So, in the hiſtory of our lives,
  The law is ſtill the ſame
A thouſand trifles make the ſum,
  Of happineſs, or pain.

Small deeds of help, small words of love,
Dropped on this path of ours
May make the rugged way all bright
With funfhine, and with flowers.

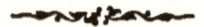

The First Decade, 1861.

————

TEN YEARS AGO, my dearest love,
  Ten years ago to-day ;
Since that bright morn, when hopefully
  We started on our way.
Joined heart, and hand, and pledged to walk
  Life's chequered journey through,
In undivided Love, and Trust,
  Firm, faithfully, and true.

Ten happy years ! tho' in their sweep
  Some changes have been cast
About our path ;—yet Love and Faith
  Have ne'er been overcast.
Care's finger, too, some deeper lines
  Upon thy brow has traced ;
And the world's harsh hands, some early dreams
  May rudely have effaced.

Yet ours has been a blefsèd lot,
  Our Sorrows have but been
Like birds of paffage, fled away,
  And left our lives ferene.
Men praife thee: and my proud heart beats
  To know through rifing Fame,
Beside our quiet hearth at home,
  Thy love is ftill the fame.

Ten years ago, we were but two,
  Now, round our lives is bound
Five-fold—a bright and flowery chain,
  Strong, circling us around.
And the glad found of Childhood's voice,
  Makes mufic in our home,
And cheers our hearts with brighteft hopes
  Of happy years to come.

God grant, dear love, the brighteft ones,
  May full fruition fee;
And Wife, and Children ever prove
  True bleffings unto thee.

And thankfully we'll raife our hearts,
To that Almighty Friend,
Who thus has bleft us, and we truft
Will blefs us to the end.

Parting Words to a Dear Brother.

———

FAREWELL, DEAR BOY, if earneft prayers,
  A thoufand in an hour,
Breathed from the hearts who love thee well,
  To Heaven's protecting power—
If warmeft wifhes can avail
  Thy future lot to blefs,
Then will thy path be bright indeed
  With life-long happinefs.

Farewell! and when thou'rt far away
  From thy dear childhood's home—
When to thy heart the tender pain
  Of memory fhall come—
Whether beneath the ftranger fky,
  Or on the deep, wild fea—
Believe, OUR fondeft memories
  Will EVER compafs THEE;

For we fhall, oft and fadly, mifs
    Thy pleafant voice and fmile,
Whofe mufic, by the hearth thou'ft left,
    Would many an hour beguile ;
Yet tho' for many weary months
    Thy vacant place we mourn,
We look, on fome bright future day,
    To hail thy bright return.

Thine onward path looks bright and fair—
    Thus may it ever be ;
And faireft hopes and brighteft dreams
    Their full fruition fee ;
And may the forrow of this hour—
    This pain of parting tears—
Be all forgotten in the fmiles
    Of future happy years.

Remember this : when upward thou
    Thy wondering glance fhall turn
To that great canopy of Heaven,
    Where tropic glories burn,

It is the fame fair fky that fhines
   Above thine own dear land,
Spread by the fame Almighty power,
   The fame protecting hand.

And to the hand of that dear God,
   We, trufting, leave thee now;
And may He lead and guide thee fafe
   Thy life's whole journey through.
Look up to Him! for in His love
   Thou fafely may'ft depend;
And then in ftorm or fhine thou'lt find
   An everlafting Friend.

Reminiscences.

OLD HOUSE! Old Home of happy years!
  I cannot pafs thee by
With carelefs fteps of unconcern,
  Or cold, indifferent eye:
I yet muft tread thy filent rooms
  With fond and clinging heart,
Though cold, and bare, and defolate,
  And tenantlefs thou art.
Strangers will hold thee for their own,
  And nevermore mine ear
Shall catch, within thy well-known porch,
  The welcome held fo dear.
Though grand in modern ftyle and tafte
  The new abode may ftand,
Though thither with glad fteps I feek
  The dear-loved houfehold band,—
Yet thy green nooks of leafy fhade,
  Thy corners quaint to fee,
Grown out of fafhion to fome eyes,
  Will ftill be dear to me.

It does not feem fo long ago
   When, to my childifh eyes,
Frefh from th' unlovely ftreets, thou wert
   A very paradife !
And fwift, beneath thine honoured roof,
   The years have fwept away,
Calmly and kind, with fcarce a fhade
   Flung o'er the pleafant way.
Changes have come : the glofly curls
   That graced our Mother's brow,
Once black as raven's ebon wing,
   Are mixed with filver now ;—
And twenty years of bufy toil,
   Have left their filent trace,
Though writ in foft and gentle lines,
   Upon our Father's face.
Beneath thy roof the neftlings grew,
   And their young wings unfurled,
Then from its fafe and pleafant fhade
   Flew forth into the world.
Yet never, never, to forget
   Their childhood's happy home,
And oft, befide its focial hearth,
   A joyful band to come.

Nor haft thou loft thy charm ; that now
 Come children not a few,
Another bright-faced band who've learned
 To know and love thee too.
This much, and more, I reverent feel
 For thee, Old Houfe, Old Home,
Such blefling has hung o'er thy roof
 That few can call their own.
With deepeft thankfulnefs to God,
 O let the words be faid,
For us thy walls have never held
 The dear, the coffined dead.
O may the fame good, gracious power
 That thus has blefled thee fo,
Alike watch over " Sunnyfide,"
 And equal gifts beftow :
For *there* are thofe who made thee dear,
 And *there* our hearts muft dwell,
Though thus I fay, with moiftened eyes,
 Old Houfe,—Old Home,—Farewell !

K

Richard Cobden,

Died April 7th, 1865.

— — —

Lo! England mourns her dead once more,
  Another noble one
Has left his place, and laid him down,
  Before his work feemed done.
Her Senate has a vacant place,
  Which through the years to come,
Will facred to his memory ftand,
  Her lateft patriot fon.

Finifhed on earth, the life twice crowned
  With glorious deeds and rare—
Achieved through long and waiting years
  Of patient toil and care.
And hufhed the voice, and ftill the lip,
  O'er which fo oft has rolled
The burning eloquence of truth,
  Refiftlefs, uncontrolled.

Great, and above earth's empty things
   Of gilded pomp and pride;
Quiet he paffed along his path,
   And unadorned he died.
Yet what will future ages tell
   Of that plain patient life,
What triumphs gained, what battles won,
   In noble bloodlefs ftrife?

Of ancient prejudice o'ercome,
   And flood-gates open hurled,
To let the tide of commerce free
   For England and the world.
While poverty took from his hands
   The boon of cheapened food—
And unborn tongues fhall echo ftill,
   " He worked his country's good."

While 'neath the pleafant country trees
   We fee him laid to reft,
And feel 'tis better he fhould fleep
   With thofe he loved the beft,

K 2

Yet the Royal Minster by the Thames
    Had been a fitting shrine,
For one who thought, and lived, and strove,
    The purest of his time.

Peace and farewell, great dead—men's strife
    Shall never pain thee more—
The peace and joy of heaven are thine
    To hold for evermore.
And humbler lives may catch from thine
    Some beams of that pure light,
Which flings a halo round thy name,
    So radiantly bright.

Abraham Lincoln,

Affassinated April 14th, 1865.

— —

A PAUSE of quiet in the ftorm,
  A dream of forrow paft,
An eager whifpering of hope
  That Peace was near at laft;
And then—Oh! who can probe the depths
  Of that recoil of pain,
When lips in horror told the tale
  Of LINCOLN bafely flain?

Dead; dead—and fwift thro' North and South
  The wail of anguifh went;
Dead! dead! "And who fhall now avenge
  The murdered Prefident?"
Afked voices breaking with the pain
  Of bitter tears unfhed,
As the awed millions gazed their laft
  Upon the martyred dead.

Laid in his last long sleep, methinks
  "Tis nothing to him now,
That Death came in such awful guise,
  To smooth his care-worn brow;
And fold the wings of heavenly Peace
  Around that honest breast,
Which burdened with it's country's woe
  Might well have longed for rest.

'Tis nothing now, what blame or praise
  The voice of man bestowed,
He trod a straight and honest path
  And left the rest with God.
And tho' his silent death-sealed lips
  Will never speak again,
The mighty echo of his voice
  For ever will remain.

That voice, which rising 'mid the storm,
  Calm, resolute and brave,
Dared to proclaim thro' blood and scorn
  The freedom of the Slave!

The present, blind, and deaf and dumb,
  It's best things may not see,
But future years will bless his name,
  Who stamped that future *free*.

He is avenged—not by the blood
  Of yon poor wasted life—
Avenged by purer, nobler things,
  Than these sad scenes of strife;
Avenged by all the manhood won
  From Slavery and Chain,
By all the joy that has eclipsed
  The memory of pain.

Avenged by all the bliss that thrills
  The mother's grateful heart,
Who knows that *now* she need not fear
  From home and babes to part.
Avenged by every bright young life
  To hope and gladness given,
By every soul *of these* redeemed
  To share the joys of heaven.

LIST OF SUBSCRIBERS.

-

THE Authoress has much pleasure in thanking her
Friends for their kind and prompt Subscription to her
little Volume, and ventures to hope that "THE TALK OF
THE HOUSEHOLD" will be a fresh link in the chain of
Friendship thus formed, and, therefore, considers it only
due to them that their names should be associated with
her humble efforts.

Her Grace the Dowager Duchess of Sutherland (6 copies).
The Right Hon. the Earl of Shaftesbury, K.G. (2 copies).
Lord Gage (2 copies).
General Garibaldi.
Signor Mazzini.
Sir Charles Roderic McGrigor, Bart. (3 copies).
Colonel G. Bruzzesi, Milan (2 copies).
Professor Newman.
Professor White.
Colonel Clementi Corti (2 copies).
John Bright, Esq., M.P.
James Stansfield, Esq., M.P.
Charles Gilpin, Esq., M.P.
Charles Seely, Esq., M.P. (4 copies).

G. J. Göschen, Esq., M.P. (2 copies).

Thomas Bayley Potter, Esq., M.P. (2 copies).

Mr. Alderman Copeland, M.P. (2 copies).

W. H. Gore Langton, Esq., M.P. (2 copies).

The Right Hon. The Lord Mayor (2 copies).

W. S. Lindsay, Esq., M.P.

Mr. Alderman Phillips (2 copies).

Mr. Alderman Abbiss (2 copies).

Mr. Alderman Lusk (2 copies).

Mr. Alderman Stone (2 copies).

Mr. Alderman Mechi.

Benjamin Scott, Esq., Chamberlain.

Wm. Corrie, Esq., Remembrancer.

Charles Warton, Esq., C.C. (2 copies).

Thomas Webber, Esq., C.C.

J. K. Farlow, Esq., C.C.

J. N. Johnson, Esq., C.C. (2 copies).

Robert Stapleton, Esq., C.C.

John Symonds, Esq., C.C.

John Thomas, Esq., C.C.

Jeremiah Coleman, Esq., C.C.

Charles John Todd, Esq., C.C.

Archibald McDougall, Esq., C.C.

Thomas Fricker, Esq., C.C.

W. Cave Fowler, Esq., C.C.

Fredk. Dadswell, Esq., C.C. (2 copies).

Robert Pallett, Esq., C.C.

G. C. Cockerell, Esq., C.C.

J. J. Blake, Esq., C.C.

Thos. Owden, Esq., Deputy (2 copies).

Charles Reed, Esq., F.S.A., C.C.
John Bennett, Esq., F.S.A., C.C. (2 copies).
W. McGeorge, Esq., C.C.
Ivie McCutchan, Esq., C.C.
S. Straker, Esq., C.C. (6 copies).
Hy. Lowman Taylor, Esq., C.C.
Edward Hart, Esq., C.C.
Mr. Deputy Obbard.
M. Hopgood, Esq., C.C.
John Walker, Esq., C.C.
David Smith, Esq., C.C.
Mrs. Czarnechi.
Matthew Noble, Esq., R.A.
Wm. Northcote, Esq., C.C.
The Rev. Dean Tighe.
Rev. Thos. Richardson, M.A. (4 copies).
Rev. Wm. Rogers, M.A. (2 copies).
Rev. Wm. Landells.
Rev. Thos. Richardson (Lancaster). (4 copies).
Montague Chambers, Esq., Q.C. (5 copies).
Mr. Sergeant Tindal Atkinson.
Thomas R. Kemp, Esq., M.A.
Edmund Beales, Esq., M.A.
John Jones, Esq., F.R.G.S.
F. G. Boutems, Esq., C.C.
Rev. Wm. Heaton, M.A. (2 copies).
Signor Volpi (*Prof. Italian, Eton College*) (3 copies)
Alfred Brett, Esq. (2 copies).
I. A. Ferris, Esq. (2 copies).
Mr. Alderman J. C. Lawrence, M.P.

Charles Rowles, Esq. (3 copies).

Professor Galloway, F.R.S. (2 copies).

Wm. Goring Pritchard, Esq.

Benjamin Clapham, Esq. (2 copies).

Robert Leeming, Esq., F.R.C.S. (2 copies).

Edmund Jackson, Esq.

Miss Adeline Cooper (2 copies).

Miss Ellen Gibson.

Mrs. Caroline Giffard Phillipson (4 copies).

Miss Catherine Swanwick (2 copies).

Miss Anna Swanwick.

Miss Leander.

Mr. Ex-Sheriff Cave.

Mrs. Cave.

Mrs. Andrew Lusk.

Mrs. G. J. Göschen (2 copies).

Mrs. C. Seely (2 copies).

Samuel Morley, Esq. (5 copies).

George Moore, Esq.

John Taylor, Esq.

Mrs. Edmond Beales.

Mrs. John Streathfield (2 copies).

Mrs. Fenning.

Miss Julia Lees.

Miss Pietroni.

Mrs. Gnitton (2 copies).

Miss Mary Minchen.

Captain D. Rogers.

D. N. Chambers, Esq., F.G.S.

Fred. Doulton, Esq., M.P. (3 copies).

Robertson Gladstone, Esq.

W. E. Foster, Esq., M.P.

E. M. Fenwick, Esq., M.P.

Rev. J. S. Workman.

Josh. Faulding, Esq.

Robert Proctor, Esq. (2 copies).

F. D. Mocatta, Esq.

Dr. Turle.

Dr. Bowron (3 copies).

S. H. Anthony, Esq.

Wm. Payne, Esq.

Mark E. Marsden, Esq.

David Chinery, Esq. (2 copies).

Mrs. David Chinery (2 copies).

B. F. Gandee, Esq.

Mrs. R. Murray (2 copies).

Samuel Plimsoll, Esq. (4 copies).

Mrs. William W. Stuart (2 copies).

Colonel Salwey (2 copies).

Edwin Andrew, Esq. (2 copies).

Josh. Morris, Esq.

Passmore Edwards, Esq.

A. F. Paxton, Esq. (2 copies).

James R. Scott, Esq.

H. L. Hammack, Esq. (2 copies).

William Dell, Esq.

J. A. Nicholay, Esq.

J. Fennings, Esq., F.R.C.S.

John Barnes, Esq.

Wm. Kingdon, Esq., Q.C.

H. M. Wilkinson, Esq.

Frederic Straker, Esq. (2 copies).

H. Bremer, Esq.

J. K. Field, Esq.

Mrs. Downing.

Daniel Taylor, Esq.

Miss Southey.

Mrs. Summerlat.

Mrs. Nathan Whitley (2 copies).

Henry Vincent, Esq. (2 copies).

Miss Dean.

Miss Isabella Fyvie.

Miss Isabella Leander.

Wm. Marshall, Esq.

Elias Davis, Esq., C.C.

Alfred J. Copeland, Esq.

Mr. Sergeant Parry (2 copies).

Hy. Long, Esq.

Richd. Barrett, Esq.

J. Sterry, Esq.

John Kaye, Esq.

John Usher, Esq.

John Corderoy, Esq.

Robt. Alex. Gray, Esq. (6 copies).

F. H. Faulding, Esq.

Mrs. Mason Jones.